2/10/05

# BUILDING with DAD

### BY CAROL NEVIUS

### ILLUSTRATED BY BILL THOMSON

mc
Marshall cavendish
children

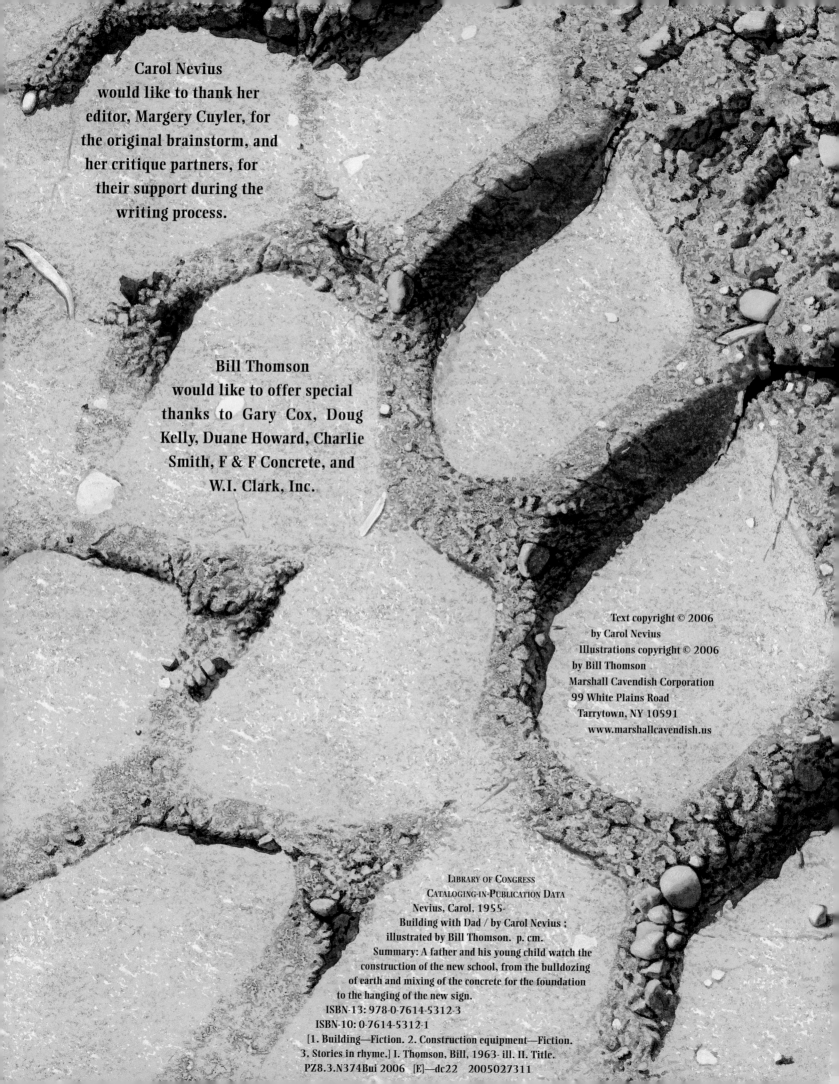

Carol Nevius would like to thank her editor, Margery Cuyler, for the original brainstorm, and her critique partners, for their support during the writing process.

Bill Thomson would like to offer special thanks to Gary Cox, Doug Kelly, Duane Howard, Charlie Smith, F & F Concrete, and W.I. Clark, Inc.

LIBRARY OF CONGRESS
CATALOGING-IN-PUBLICATION DATA
Nevius, Carol, 1955-
Building with Dad / by Carol Nevius ;
illustrated by Bill Thomson.  p. cm.
Summary: A father and his young child watch the
construction of the new school, from the bulldozing
of earth and mixing of the concrete for the foundation
to the hanging of the new sign.
ISBN-13: 978-0-7614-5312-3
ISBN-10: 0-7614-5312-1
[1. Building—Fiction. 2. Construction equipment—Fiction.
3. Stories in rhyme.] I. Thomson, Bill, 1963- ill. II. Title.
PZ8.3.N374Bui 2006  [E]—dc22  2005027311

The text of this book is set in Ellington MT.
The illustrations are rendered in acrylic paint and
colored pencil on hot press watercolor board.

Book design by Michael Nelson

Printed in China
First edition

1 3 5 6 4 2

**mc Marshall Cavendish**
Children

A portion of the proceeds from
the sale of *Building with Dad* will
be donated to the American Library
Association's Hurricane Katrina fund.

*This book is dedicated with love
to my parents, John and Beatrice Nevius,
my rock-strong foundation.*
—C.N.

*This book is dedicated
to my best friend and greatest inspiration—
my beautiful wife, Diann.*
—B.T.

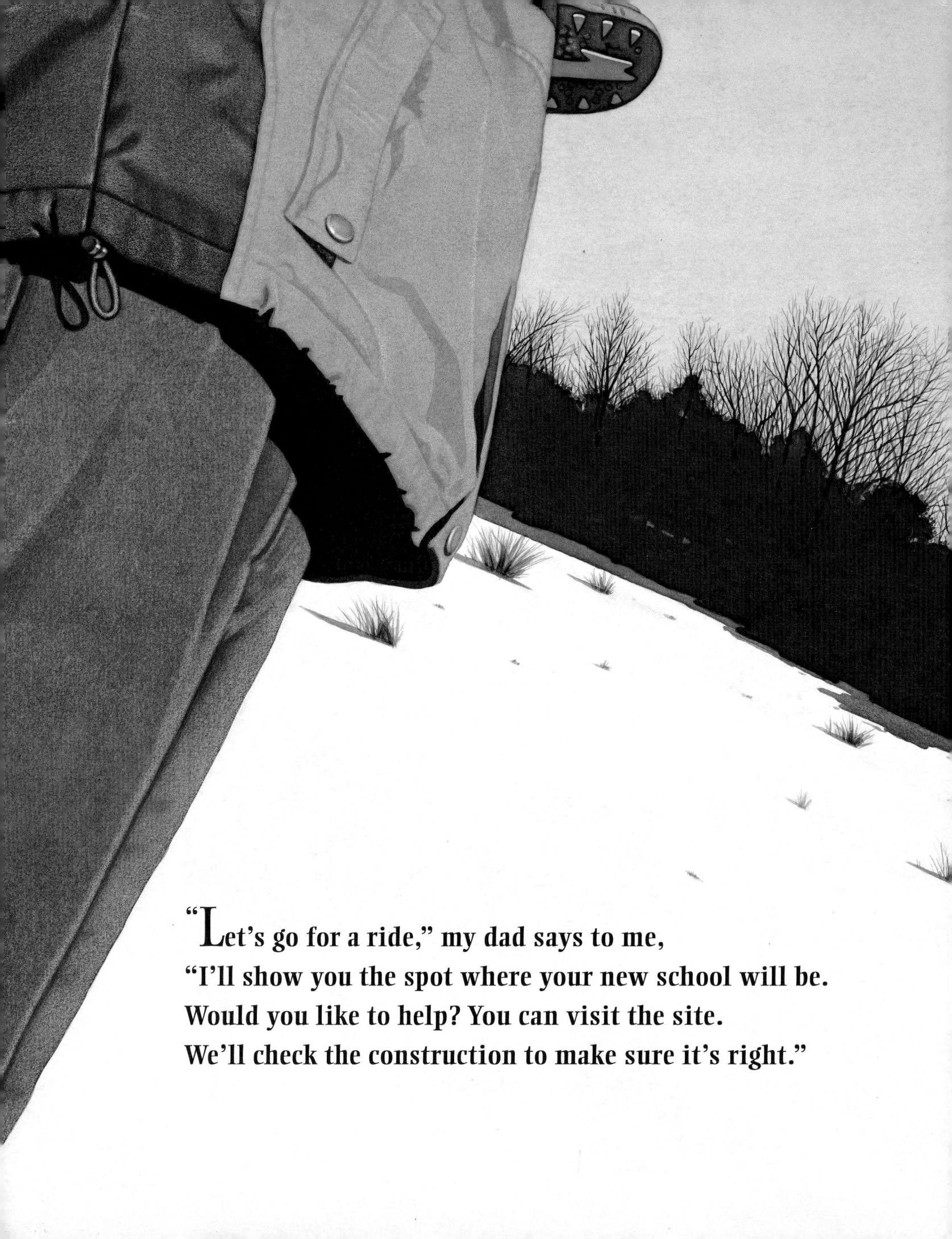

"Let's go for a ride," my dad says to me,
"I'll show you the spot where your new school will be.
Would you like to help? You can visit the site.
We'll check the construction to make sure it's right."

We wait till the groundbreaking work has begun.
Watch bulldozers ROAR. Pushing dirt, diesels run.

We ride in the dump truck that's bringing in fill.
I push the red button to make the rocks spill!

I help Dad's mechanic. We count all her wrenches,
and watch as the backhoe digs long pipeline trenches.

At noon, horns TOOT-TOOT! The crew needs to eat.
Dad lets me climb up in the earthmover's seat!

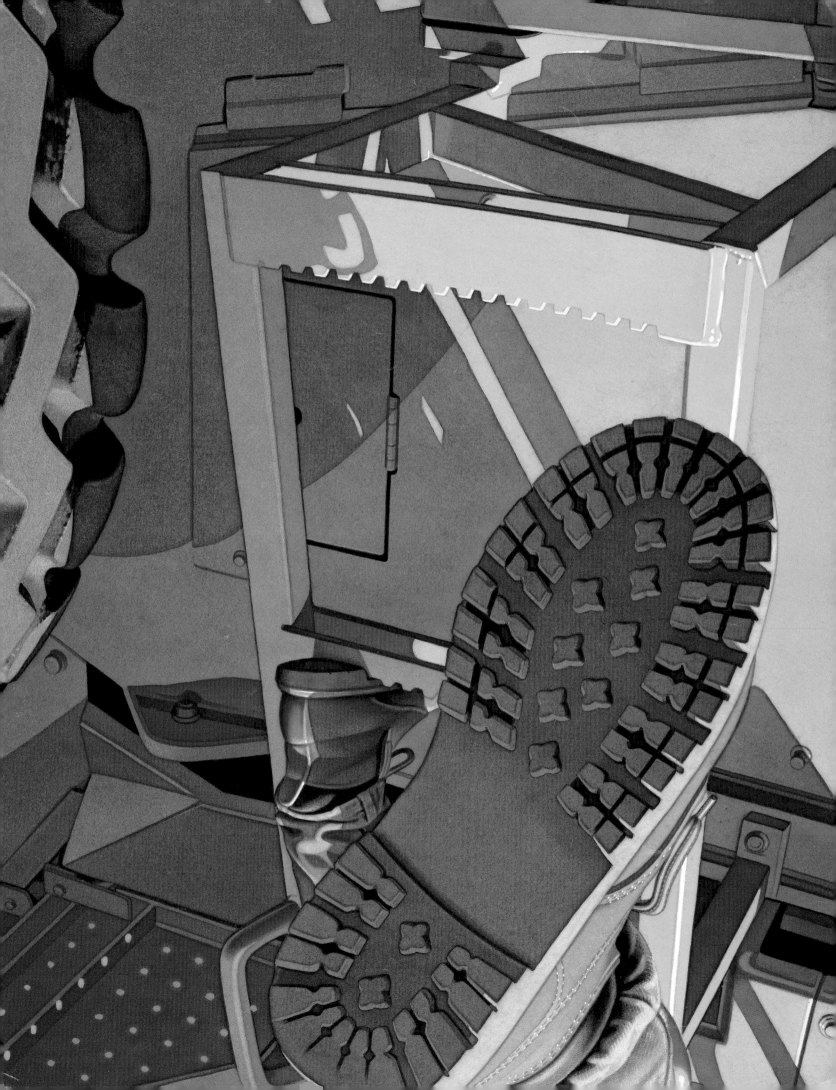

Dad's giant grader smoothes over the ground.
His steamroller follows to crush the dirt down.

Cement mixer turns out gray glop by the yard.
The foundation forms. It sets up and dries hard.

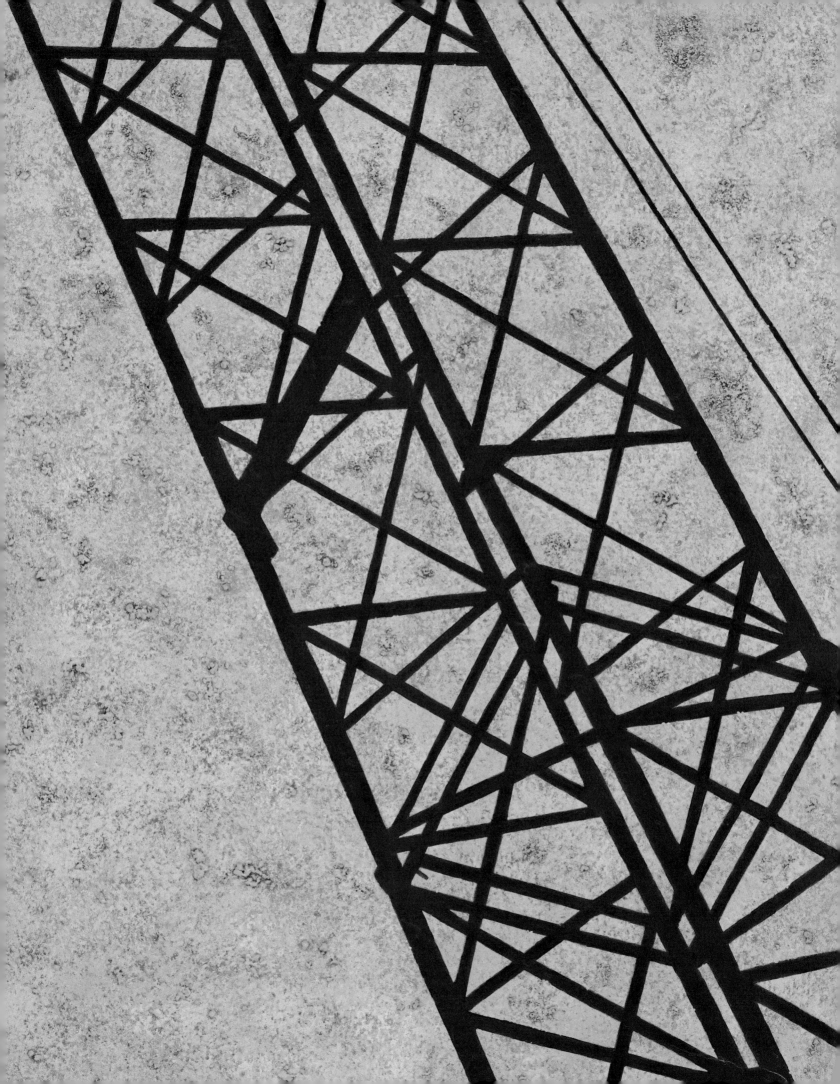

Cranes are like arms, lifting girders and brick.
Crews bolt, nut, and mortar them, solid and thick.

Zip-zap! The power tools fasten the ply.
The new roof is waterproof. School will be dry.

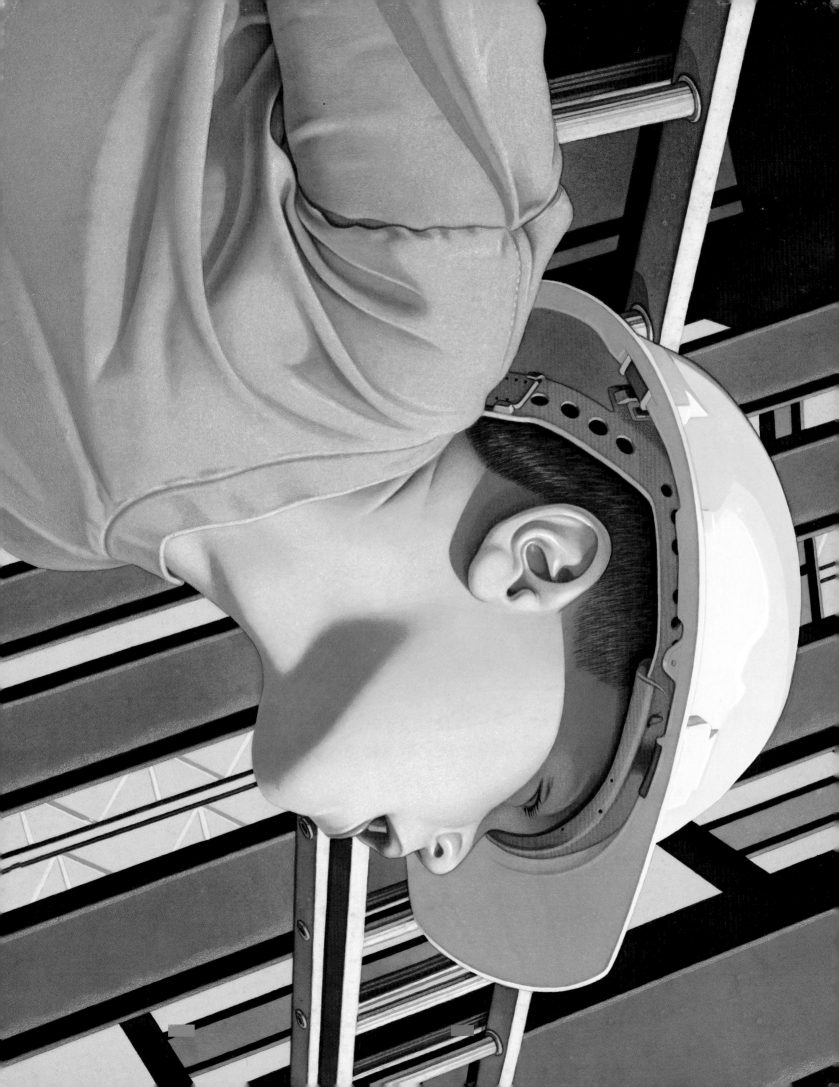

The frames are the rib bones, a skeleton wall,
outlining the classrooms, the gym, and the hall.

The team works inside, welding pipes using fire,
sealing windows and tile, running cables and wire.

The teachers have meetings. Dad's last workers rush.
Our waxed floors are gleaming. The toilets all flush.

The bucket truck lifts us to check the new sign.
I spell out each letter. I'm proud this school's mine!

Construction is finished. Dad packs his last tool.
The children arrive. It's the first day of school!

And when I'm a grown-up, I hope I will be
a builder like Dad with a helper like me!